*W*hen a **Dragon** *Goes to School*

First published 2020 by Nosy Crow Ltd
The Crow's Nest, 14 Baden Place
Crosby Row, London SE11YW
www.nosycrow.com

ISBN 978 1 78800 770 2 (HB)
ISBN 978 1 78800 771 9 (PB)

Nosy Crow and associated logos are trademarks
and/or registered trademarks of Nosy Crow Ltd.

Text © Caryl Hart 2020
Illustrations © Rosalind Beardshaw 2020

The rights of Caryl Hart to be identified as the author and of Rosalind Beardshaw
to be identified as the illustrator of this work have been asserted.

A CIP catalogue record for this book is available from the British Library.

Printed in China

Papers used by Nosy Crow are made from wood grown in sustainable forests.

10 9 8 7 6 5 4 3 2 1 (HB)
10 9 8 7 6 5 4 3 2 1 (PB)

For Kat. Love you! Mum xx
C. H.

To Carley and Lotte,
with love, Rosi x
R. B.

When a Dragon Goes to School

Caryl Hart
Rosalind Beardshaw

When a **dragon** hears us say . . . .

. . . "HOORAY! We're off to **school** today!"

Does she refuse to come inside
or try to run away and hide?

Why, no! Dragons don't do that!

A dragon **scampers** through the gate,
then waves goodbye – she's never late.
She **shakes** the raindrops from her wings,
then takes off all her outdoor things
and hangs them nice and tidily.

That's just how dragons **are**, you see.

And after she has said, "Hello!"
a dragon knows just where to go.

She sits down in her special place,
a dragon **smile** across her face.
She's ready to begin the day.

These things are just a dragon's **way**.

Then when it's time to paint and draw,
does this young dragon use a paw

to **decorate** her little chair,
or **toss** the crayons in the air?

Why, no! Dragons don't do that!

A dragon hands the paper out.
She doesn't make a mess or shout.
She counts the pencils – one, two, three,
then draws a rainbow carefully
and paints it red and green and blue.

All dragons love bright things – do you?

At lunch, a dragon is polite
and **never** takes too big a bite.
This small, kind darling saves a space
and extra lunchtime snacks, in case
a friend would like a tasty treat.

Yes, dragons really are that sweet!

But in the playground, does she whine,
or hog the trike and shout out, "Mine!"?

Does this small dragon play too rough,
or **march** off in a grumpy huff?

Why, no! Dragons don't do that!

A dragon **shares** the outdoor toys
with other little girls and boys.
Her dragon dance is **so** much fun,
she's always friends with everyone
who wants to join her dragon romp.

Would **you** enjoy a dragon stomp?

When **splashing** in the water tray,
this little dragon laughs away,

and if her playmates are upset
because their clothes are getting wet,
she'll help them tie their apron strings.

All dragons do such thoughtful things.

But if the day feels overlong,
that's when a dragon might go wrong.
So tidy up the classroom, then
get **comfy** in the reading den
and lose yourselves inside a book.

This dragon **loves** a story . . . look!

At home time, does a dragon **shout**
and try to get the books back out,

or **growl** and **howl** with all her might,
while clinging to the teacher tight?

Why, no! Dragons don't do that!

A dragon **knows** the day must end,
so says goodbye to every friend.
She wraps a scarf around her throat
and finds her bookbag and her coat,
then **skips** out to her family.

How **perfect** can a dragon be?

And if she **roars** along the street
and stamps her little dragon feet,

"More school! **More school!**"
you'll hear her call,

well . . .

she is a dragon after all!